Lady Lindsay

Lyrics and Other Poems

Lady Lindsay

Lyrics and Other Poems

ISBN/EAN: 9783744777421

Printed in Europe, USA, Canada, Australia, Japan

Cover: Foto ©Andreas Hilbeck / pixelio.de

More available books at **www.hansebooks.com**

LYRICS,

AND

OTHER POEMS,

BY

LADY LINDSAY.

LONDON

KEGAN PAUL, TRENCH, TRÜBNER & CO., Ltd.

MDCCCXC

TO

THE MEMORY OF

MY MOTHER.

OF these poems, none have been hitherto published, except the following:—"A Child Flower," "The East Neuk," and "Lavender," which appeared in "Atalanta," "A Woman's Story" in the "English Illustrated Magazine," "Her Last Letter" in "Macmillan's Magazine," and "Robin in Winter" in "About Robins."

CONTENTS.

THE FIELD-WORKERS.

ALL day long we toil and labour,
  Sow or garner, delve or reap,
Yet there comes a time, my neighbour,
  When we rest before we sleep.
Then, and whatsoe'er the weather,
  Be it early, be it late,
For a while we stand together,
  Lingering at my garden gate.

Oft you bring a rose or pansy—
  By your wall they bloom the best—
Hearts grow soft and kind, I fancy,
  When the sun sinks in the west !
Oft, to make good-night the surer,
  You repeat it at your door ;
Whilst my poor home seems the poorer,
  As I lift the latch once more.

So, you've thought my life too lonely?
　　Nay, God knows what's best for me.
You've one bright-haired darling only;
　　See, she climbs up on my knee!
She's half mine already, (bless her!)
　　Say, can her dead mother mind
If I tend the child, wash, dress her?
　　She knows that I'm not unkind.

Well, we'll marry; take and hold it,
　　This brown hand as seared as yours.
Here, in this hard north, of old it
　　Seems we women brought such dowers.
Let us love as well as labour;
　　Side by side we'll delve or reap;
Then, when we've grown old, dear neigh-
　　　　bour,
　　We may rest before we sleep!

FROM A WINDOW.

THERE'S a prisoned blackbird over the
    way;
  His cage hangs on the wall,
  And his horizon small
Shows him the London brickwork night
    and day.

And yet he sings, ah ! he gaily sings,
  Of green lanes, of green trees,
  The sun, the summer breeze,
A summer love, and all delightful things.

So we—though cruelly held and tied—
  Within our songs may weave
  That which we love, believe,
Or hope, or dream, and all sweet thoughts
    beside.

THE LONELY FELL.

THE daylight fades, the road is steep,
    The mist is wreathing fast;
Then haste thee, traveller, if ere night
    Thy journey should be past.
'Tis years ago since first I came,
    Alone, thus here to dwell;
By day, by night, I strain mine eyes
    To gaze across the fell;
And yet I'm fain to gaze in vain
    Across the lonely fell.

'Tis years ago—I met him here,
    Here on the silent heath;
Upon my brow I felt his kiss,
    Upon my cheek his breath.

'Twas but a moment—then he turned:
    " Dear heart, a short farewell !"
Nay, for the years have come and gone
    Like shadows on the fell ;
And yet I'm fain to gaze in vain
    Across the lonely fell.

A CHILD FLOWER.

ONLY a sick child peering down
  At a narrow court and the world's sad
    ills;
Only a poor little pallid child,
  Holding a nosegay of daffodils.

I saw her there in her thin black gown,
  Leaning far out on the window-sill;
And, as I look'd up with a pitiful smile,
  She smil'd, and she threw me a daffodil.

Her fair hair shone like the crown of gold
  Such brave little martyrs may wear in
    heav'n,
To whom in this cruel dark city of ours
  Sorrow and suff'ring are freely giv'n.

*   *   *   *   *

A month ago I pass'd down the street;

  'Twas crowded and busy at close of

    day—

But yon window was shut, and the blind

    was drawn,

  And I sigh'd as I went once more on

    my way.

THE PEARL GATHERER.

'Tis there—where the blue billows curl
    In the perfum'd warm east,
Where, rapturous, meet sun and spray,
    Whilst the breeze plays the priest;
Where life's but a languid sweet day—
There the diver leaps for the pearl.

But below—in the twilight-bound deep,
    In the solemn cold shade,
Where never a sound is heard,
    Where he shrinks, half afraid,
From creatures that glare as they're
       stirr'd—
His harvest of pearl he'll reap.

For he who a gem would find,

   A treasure not bought,

Must leave the sun for the gloom,

   And in stillness of thought,

Standing calm before possible doom,

Reign alone o'er the realm of his mind.

A WOMAN'S STORY.

Ay, 'twas thirty year ago—
All the garden was aglow:
Ruddy holyoaks, red roses,
Marigold and salvia posies,
Stately sunflow'rs, humble pansies—
"Heart's-ease true as little Nan's is,"
Quoth my lover, speaking low.
In the orchard trilled a robin.
Ah me! how my heart was throbbin',
Those long happy years ago!

Well, the tale's been often told:
Two things, pure love and pure gold,
Do not wane with passing fashion.
Life's cold without human passion.
Pick me that blue pansy yonder—

Thoughts for pansies, say you?—fonder
Grow our thoughts as we wax old.
Haply, as the rough path steepens,
And our feet lag, true love deepens—
Just because the tale's retold.

THE EAST NEUK.

'Tis a soft west wind, and no mist is in the
air,
And the herring-boats go sailing, sailing,
sailing far away,
Sailing fast and free
To the mighty open sea,
To the wide and golden east that lies
shining over there.

On the fresh green links we will sit awhile
and rest,
Whilst the boats shoot from the pier-head
and go sailing far away ;
Loud their brave men cheer,
Watching homesteads dear

And kirk and harbour-bar slide back, and
faces loved the best.

At the red gabled roofs from our height
we can look down,
Whilst beyond with silver track the boats
go sailing far away;
Now only women bide
To mind the fireside,
And only children's voices ring within the
quiet town.

'Mong seaweed-spread fields the barefoot
lassies hoe,
Whilst the herring-boats go sailing, sailing,
sailing far away,
Through firth and northern seas,
T'ward Orkney and Hebrides—
God bless the hardy fishers who o'er stormy
waters go !

"QUEENE OF THE MEDOWES."

MEADOW sweet, my meadow sweet,
Grown so lithe about my feet,
Wild and free,
Under birch and under beech,
Pure and kind as Nature's speech,
Fair to see !

Meadow sweet, my meadow sweet,
City walls can ne'er be meet,
Dear, for thee !
Should I take thee from thy glade,
And bid thee bloom in prison'd shade?
Nay, let be.

YEARS AFTER.

I AM going home to our village,
  Yon village beside the sea,
And my heart outcries with the memories
  That float in, with the tide, to me.

I stand 'neath the silver moonlight,
  My feet in the curling foam,
And there rises a spell that I know right
    well,
  From the waves and the boats and home.

My father 's long dead, and my mother;
  And he, whom I loved yet more,
One night sailed forth to the darkening
    north
  As he'd sailed out so oft before.

I prayed—I was sick with waiting—
    That he'd come and thus ease my pain ;
But news spread from town how the ship
       had gone down,
    And my waiting was all in vain.

They told me the tale in the evening,
    As I sat on the yellow sands
Where oft we had walked, and lingered,
       and talked,
    And clung to each other's hands.

Above me the white clouds are scudding,
    Like sails on a deep blue main ;
Oh ! the winds blow strong where my true
       love so long
    In his cold wet grave has lain !

OF A RING.

A VERY little thing
Is this, a wedding-ring,
Yet much of joy or sorrow can it bring.

Within such margin round
Two fates are closely wound,
Two souls are one unto the other bound.

Herein lies paradise,
To every she that's wise,
Whilst he finds heav'n reflected in her eyes.

It seems a burden light,
A bond they'd wish more tight,
As long as each in other finds delight:

c

A fetter far too strong,

A weight to drag along,

When vice or folly bid the heart do wrong.

THE KING'S DAUGHTER.

HAIL, the king's daughter from over the
    sea !
Fair as the heath on the mountain is she ;
Pale as the lilies that grow in the wold ;
Crown'd with her tresses of dusky gold.

Hail the king's daughter from over the
    sea !
The barons are kneeling on bended knee
As she passes along, serene and tall,
Through the joyous throng in the great
    old hall.

*   *   *   *   *

The king doth stand on her fair right
    hand;
  Her maidens are at her side;
Her pages are bearing her broider'd train
  With a grave and conscious pride.

The minstrel sings, the castle rings
  With the sound of mirth and glee,
And outside the gate the people wait
  The fair young queen to see.

Yet her eyes are dim, and they fill to the
    brim
  At the thought of what ne'er may be,
And her heart grows cold with a longing
    untold
  For the land that lies over the sea.

MOTHER'S VISION.

A LITTLE child's face, at the dead of night,
That comes to me, enwrapt in wondrous
     light,
A little child's fair presence that doth seem
Gladly familiar—ah, my heart, I dream,
     I dream, alas ! I dream.

A little child's step that, with hasty tread,
Crosses the floor—a touch upon my bed—
Bright wide blue eyes that never learned
     to weep,
A red mouth laughing—ah, my heart, I
     sleep,
     I sleep, alas ! I sleep.

A little child's kiss—now a murmured sigh,

A word almost—nay, this is not good-bye ;

I cannot spare thee ! not for thy dear sake,

Nor mine, nor any—ah, my heart, I wake,

I wake, alas ! I wake !

HER LAST LETTER.

'Tis but a line, a hurried scrawl,
   And little seem the words to say,
Yet hold me in reproachful thrall:
   "You quarrelled with me yesterday;
      To-morrow you'll be sad."

Ay, "you'll be sad," the words are few,
   And yet they pierce my soul with pain;
Ay, "you'll be sad," the words are true;
   They haunt me with prophetic strain:
      "To-morrow you'll be sad."

We quarrelled—and for what? A word,
   An idle speech that jarred the ear,

And thus in wrath our pulses stirr'd ;
   Then came her letter : " Dear, my dear,
      To-morrow you'll be sad."

Writ half in mirth, half in regret,
   Last words that she should ever write,
Learn'd long ago, and yet, and yet,
   Fraught with new pain to ear and sight :
      " To-morrow you'll be sad."

BEYOND.

Do you know

Where the dear swallows go,

When winter is near and chill winds blow ?

Afar they fly,

In blue ether, so high

That we cannot follow their course through

the sky.

Yet in unknown lands of warmth and light

They live, and forget our winter's night.

Do you know

Where the dear children go,

When summer fades and chill Death waits ?

They soar beyond
Thoughts tender and fond,
And watch for our coming at Heaven's
gates.

And haply, in worlds outside our ken,
They pity the earthly sorrows of men.

A RHYME OF ARCADY.

SHEPHERD lads and lasses,
  Come and trip in the dew;
Come through woodland passes,
  Come unto pastures new.
Come and dance in the merry moonlight,
For winds are soft and the stars are bright.

Shepherd lads and lasses,
  Now your sheep are in fold,
Come and pluck sweet grasses,
  And wander across the wold;
Or sit and pipe to your Valentines,
Under the shade of the murmuring pines.

FIRESIDE.

Gazing into the fire,
 With baby on my knee,
Ere the crimson coals expire,
 How many things I see !

Into the future peering,
 To read what life shall be ;
How much I'm hoping, fearing,
 For the babe upon my knee !

AN OLD BOOK.

An old torn book, with one pale rose
  Crushed in its yellow pages :
I have not held it in my hand,
  Nor read it thus, for ages.

Nay, formerly, the print was good ;
  Or else mine eyes were better,
For now they're full of tears—too full
  To see a single letter !

MY BROTHER AND I.

Half hid in mist of time and many tears,
  Stands the French ruined castle by the
    sea,
  On a green hill, from whence so often
    we,
Hand locked in hand, gazed out across
    the years
Toward a future of unmeasured space—
A future fair as ocean's placid face.

Then he, my brother, passed beyond, to
    where
  Death's great gate shuts out heav'n from
    earthly eyes,
  Whilst I lived on, to learn, with sad
    surprise,

How man's injustice mars this lovely
    sphere.

And yet, methinks, we both like children
    stand

And bridge our sundered fates with clasp-
    ing hand.

THE DUSTMAN.

I WELL recal how oft my mother said :
" Farewell, dear sweet ! 'tis time to go to
  bed.
Pray kiss good-night without a word or
  sigh ;
I see the dustman plainly in your eye !"

Who might that dustman be ? I never
  learned.
His phantom company in wrath I spurned ;
My blue eyes oped as wide as they would go,
His absence most convincingly to show.

Yet life brings changes. Oft, in weary
  hours,

I'd fain be bound by childhood's chain of
    flowers ;
I'd cry : " Dear friends, behold ! the dust-
    man see
Here, in mine eye, as plain as plain can
    be ! "

One day our lids must droop, whate'er our
    will,
One day our hearts must lie quite cold,
    quite still ;
That dustman weird, called Sleep in
    childish days,
At last named Death, shall from our dim
    eyes gaze.

MORNING.

Fly away unto the sun,
O thou early-rising lark !
Fly o'er meadow, moor, and park,
Now the day has just begun,
While such idle folks as I
On their downy pillows lie.

Fly away unto the north,
O thou brown-sailed fisher boat,
That so merrily dost float
On the silver-crested Forth !
While such foolish folks as I
At the window stand and sigh.

Fly away unto the clouds,
O my sorrow-laden thought !

There, perchance, shalt thou be wrought

Into rain or misty shrouds;

While such lonely folks as I

From their aching hearts outcry.

TO A BABY.

BABY, what vague thoughts arise
    In your eyes,
As you sit, red lips asunder,
    And in wonder
Gaze round at your untried world,
    Just unfurl'd?

Baby, you who come from Heaven,
    And are given
Great grave thoughts, this world's so little,
    Scarce one tittle
But will make you grieve and sigh,
    By and bye.

Baby, if our hopes may clear
    This dull sphere,

Change not. Be at long life's ending,

Homeward wending,

Angel-led to God again,

Free from stain.

SUMMER VOWS.

ALL among the golden corn,
    Summer vows are spoken ;
All amid the winter snow,
    Summer vows are broken.
Youth and Summer both go by ;
Haply we may sit and sigh,
    From our dreams awoken !

LITTLE THINGS.

A LITTLE song springs from a well of sorrow,

A little cloud brings heavy rain to-morrow,

A little love much after-grief doth borrow:

Child, child, deem not this world too hard,

Nor that thou wrongly art debarr'd

From aught—thou hast thy human dower

Of love and tears, thy life's short hour.

FOAM FANCY.

OVER the sea,
In days long ago,
There came a white ship
From a land of snow.

It brought to the children
A bushel of toys,
It brought to the grown folks
Sweet blessings and joys.

It brought to all sad hearts
A message of peace,
And to some weary pilgrims
A word of release.

It brought to the poet

The song he loved best—

So begins the old legend;

I know not the rest.

THE FIDDLER'S FIDDLE.

THERE lived an old fiddler called Jinks,
    Who dwelt by the town's high wall;
He played in the morning, at noon and at
      night,
    He fiddled to great and small.
And, e'en as his fingers flew over the strings,
    He murmured this weary song:
"Oh why, and oh why, is a man's life short,
    When the life of a fiddle 's so long?"

His house was uncared-for, his garden
      grew waste,
    All empty his money-bags;
His children went barefoot, his dinner was
      scant,
    And his clothes hung in tatters and rags;

But still, as he fiddled and fiddled away,
    He sighed out his weary song:
" Oh why, and oh why, is a man's life short,
    When the life of a fiddle 's so long?"

He died, and his grandson—a noble
    youth—
    Rose up in the old man's place;
He played the old viol, and handled the
    bow
    With vigour and deftness and grace.
Yet folks as they listened, entranced and
    amazed,
    Remembered that weary song:
"Oh why, and oh why, is a man's life short,
    When the life of a fiddle 's so long?"

A FAIRY TALE.

A PRINCESS dwelt in a high white tower,
  A very long time ago,
And that she grew up and bloomed like a
    flower
  I'm perfectly sure you know.

One day there rode from a distant land
  A king of mighty renown;
He came, as you'll guess, to sue for her
    hand,
  And offer his heart and crown.

Then a second king, from over the sea,
  Came sailing through cloud and mist;

He knelt to the princess on bended knee,
  And her lily-white hand he kiss'd.

But to each of those monarchs she said :
    " Nay, nay,
  The prince of my thoughts will come ;
He must come to-morrow if not to-day,
  And carry me back to his home."

He came ; his armour was ruddy gold,
  His hair like the sunset rays.
Of the three he was youngest and best,
    we're told—
  They all lived to the end of their days.

A PHANTASY.

Sailing, sailing,
Over the sea—
Who will come
In a ship with me?

Out and beyond
To the starry East,
When the night is past,
And the storm has ceased.

Or drifting down
To the languid South,
Where the silver waves flow
To the broad river's mouth.

Or afar, afar
To the ice-bound North,
Where the weird snow-men
To battle go forth.

Or away and away
To the golden West,
Where the King of the Sunbeams
Has gone to his rest.

MOTHER'S SONG.

COME to thy nest,
Close to my breast,
Baby, dearest Baby;
Here, on its bed,
Lay thy sweet head,
Cosily as may be.

Curl thy soft arm,
Careless and warm,
Around my neck and shoulder;
Ah, how we miss
Mother's fond kiss,
Baby, when we're older !

WHEN I WAS YOUNG.

When I was young, the world was fair—
    (Sing, Marjorie,)
Now seems it dark and full of care,
And I must many a burden bear—
    Ah me! Ah me!

Folks smiled on me in days bygone—
    (Sing, Marjorie,)
Now may I sit and make my moan,
Or, if I smile, smile all alone—
    Ah me! Ah me!

Farewell sweet days, so far, so near—
    (Sing, Marjorie,)

E

No future like the past is dear,
No future shines so bright and clear—
Ah me! Ah me!

A ROMANCE.

A LITTLE maid sat sewing,
   On the doorstep sewèd she :
" I'll bide me here till the hot noon's near,
   And my love rides back to me."

He came.   It was chilly evening;
   The tears from her eyelids fell;
But when he drew nigh the teardrops grew
      dry—
   And there's nothing more to tell.

THE EXILE.

Swallow, swallow, from over the sea,

What is the song thou art bringing for me?

What are the tidings thy sweet presence

bears?

Tenderest chidings, and longings, and

prayers?

Swallow, swallow, from over the sea,

Give me the message was given to thee!

Swallow, swallow, from lands far away,

Tell me, what words did my dear ones say?

Though here I am lonely their eyes watch

for me,

Gazing and yearning across the wide sea.

Swallow, swallow, from lands far away,

Bring me the thoughts of my loved ones

to-day!

LOVE'S MUSIC.

I.

Love thought one day to sing a lay—
  He sang (poor foolish boy !)
Of love's delight and happiness,
  Fond troth and lover's joy ;
Of hearts that grow to be as one,
  Twin souls as fair as flow'rs,
And all the bliss that love can bring
  Upon this world of ours.

But they that listened sneer'd or sighed,
  And many turn'd away ;
For there were some who could not tell
  What Love had meant to say.

Then Love was fain to sing again—
　　He tuned his lute anew :
The long weird chords thrill'd in the air,
　　And piercèd all hearts through.
He sang of love, and lover's grief,
　　Sad troth, and silent woe,
Of all the pain that love can bring
　　Upon this world below.

And, as he sang, the people wept
　　Because of that sweet lay ;
For there were none who could not tell
　　What Love had meant to say.

SONNET

(SUGGESTED BY MR. WATTS' PICTURE OF
LOVE AND DEATH).

YEA, Love is strong as life; he casts out
    fear,
And wrath, and hate, and all our envious
    foes;
He stands upon the threshold, quick to
    close
The gate of happiness ere should appear
Death's dreaded presence—ay, but Death
    draws near,
And large and grey the towering outline
    grows,
Whose face is veil'd and hid; and yet
    Love knows
Full well, too well, alas! that Death is
    here.

Death tramples on the roses ; Death comes
　　in,
Though Love, with outstretch'd arms and
　　wings outspread,
Would bar the way—poor Love, whose
　　wings begin
To droop, half-torn as are the roses dead
Already at his feet—but Death must win,
And Love grows faint beneath that
　　ponderous tread !

A CAROL.

Ring the bells,

Ring the bells,

Ring the merry Christmas bells ;

And let their voice resound,

Around, around,

Till o'er the leas and o'er the fells,

The gladsome echo loudly tells

How we to-day

Are blithe and gay,

And how for all sad hearts we pray.

Ring the bells,

Ring the bells,

Ring the joyful Christmas bells !

Ring the bells,

Ring the bells,

Ring the merry Christmas bells.
　So ring them high and low,
　　O'er ice and snow,
O'er craggèd hills and sombre dells,
While round the earth the message swells
　　How we to-day
　　Are blithe and gay,
And how for all sad hearts we pray.
　　Ring the bells,
　　Ring the bells,
Ring the joyful Christmas bells !

A CHRISTMAS FANCY.

THERE dwelt a little sprite
    In a belfry high,
    Up close to the sky,
  And there, by day and night,
He heard the big bells clang with ever-new
    delight.

He was a shrewish thing,
    On mischief bent
    With a wild intent;
  The bells he loved to ring,
But mostly was he glad discord and dread
    to bring.

At times there passed a sound
    Of melody faint,

As though a saint
Sang low ; folks stood spell-bound,
Then on a sudden gasped—for silence
reigned around.

Yet, when in church there pealed
The organ loud,
And the reverent crowd
Hymned praise, or meekly kneeled—
Down came a hideous din, as though fiends
fought and skrceled.

It was the elf, no doubt—
So wise men said,
With shake of head ;
And maids scarce ventured out
When storm-winds blew, lest evil luck
should come about.

And far away at sea,
In evening late,
The mariner's fate
Wailed itself plaintively
From that same belfry tower girt by an ivy
tree.

And children screamed for naught;
And peaceful men,
Now and agen,
Heard battle-sounds loud fraught
With stirring trumpet-calls, and left their
homes distraught.

Thus homely folks were dazed;
And all the while,
With wicked smile,
The sprite peered down half-crazed,
Because of joy to make this silly world
amazed.

Only on Christmas morn—
Ay, once a year—
He bent his ear
And shrank back all forlorn,
Whilst o'er the vale the bells' sweet carol-
ling was borne.

At every Christmas tide
He was undone :
His power right gone.
When peace on earth doth stay,
'Tis angels ring the bells—for thus the
peasant people say.

DURING ILLNESS.

IF it should please the Lord I die,

And lie

Beneath the greensward calm and still—

His will

Be mine without regret or sigh.

Yet if it please the Lord I stay

To-day,

And meet once more the din and strife

Of life—

Content, I'll arm me for the fray.

HUMAN LITTLENESS.

BE thou content to leave thy life, thy fate,
    In guidance to thy Maker;
Of all this mighty world wherein thou art
    Thou canst not shift one acre.

The world rolls on, the seasons come and
    go,
    Thy will decides no tittle;
And for thy future, be it good or ill,
    Thou may'st decree as little.

*   *   *

God's will be done,
He knows what's best;
Finish duty begun,
Leave Him the rest !

SONGS OF NATURE.

IN THE WOODS.

I LOVE to roam in the woods
When the green leaves are dying,
I love to roam in the woods
Where the brown leaves are lying,
And see the wild dove on the wing,
And hear the tuneful robin sing :
"'Tis autumn, 'tis autumn, 'tis golden
autumn now,
But soon cometh winter, with cold winds
and snow."

I love to roam in the woods
When the dead leaves are falling,
I love to roam in the woods
Where the wood-nymphs are calling,

And hear the chant of goblin men

Who gather fuel in the glen :

" 'Tis autumn, 'tis autumn, 'tis golden

autumn now,

But soon cometh winter, with cold winds

and snow."

THE COMING OF SPRING.

STERN Winter reigns—a tyrant king—
He bids the rough winds rave and blow,
And builds us prison-walls of snow.
But Spring,
Green-girdled Spring, comes surely;
And in her pride of youth
Knowing nor love nor ruth,
Shall bind him down securely.

He will not yield in anything
To that usurper—let him die!
For him will no man grieve or sigh.
But Spring,
Triumphant Spring, shall glory;
So bid the earth rejoice,
And let the merry voice
Of birds proclaim the story!

AMONG THE WATER WAYS.

WHERE the green reeds bend and quiver
On the narrow winding river,
  There I'll moor my boat at noon:
Where the sunbeams glint and shiver,
  Prisoned by the darkness soon.

Deep down where the water eddies,
Where the moor-hen's silent bed is,
  There I'll dream long hours away:
By the lilies in the sedges,
  Where the tiny ripples play.

Round and round within the hollows
O'er the water skim the swallows,
  Flying, flying fast and low:
And the light wind softly follows,
  And the reeds bend to and fro.

RICHMOND PARK IN OCTOBER.

THE tawny oaks, despite wild winds that
    sear,
  Yet keep their leaves; clear is the
    distant view;
Across the face of heav'n doth not appear
  One cloud or speck to mar the peaceful
    blue.

Th' unfrighted deer, 'mong golden bracken
    strayed,
  Scarce turn to watch our footsteps on
    the grass;
Like flecks of sunshine scattered in the
    glade
  Down to the sapphire water-streak they
    pass.

The city lies out yonder—there folks go
  And come, opprest with stir and din of
    life,
Although so near fresh hawthorn-berries
  grow,
  The sweet birds sing, the world seems
    free from strife.

For here is shed a beauty o'er the scene,
  To nature as to us by autumn brought :
Time's deepening glow—grave tender
    thoughts between—
  And days of strength of which our
    youth knew naught.

THE WIND AND THE SEA.

I SAT beside the shore, and heard the
    voice of the wind :
  "O mighty sea, why sleepest thou?
  Arouse thee, I am here, why sleepest
    now?
  I come, and with me follow far behind
  The rains and storms to which the
    earth shall bow."

I sat beside the shore, and heard the
    voice of the sea :
  "O mighty wind, why art thou here?
  Why didst thou leave thy hills and
    clouds, to peer
  Into my slumbers, and awaken me?
  Begone! I rave and rage when thou
    art near!"

ROBIN IN WINTER.

A BIRD flew out from the green holly
    hedge,
    And sang me a sweet song to-day;
Beside me he perched on the white
    window-ledge,
    And carolled his innocent lay.
With a hey and a ho, sang my pretty
    Robin low:
"There's somebody coming at Christmas,
    you know."

The sun shone out and the clouds went
    by,
    The wind died softly away;

A joy seemed spread over earth and sky,
  And my heart grew tender and gay.
With a hey and a ho, sang my pretty
    Robin low :
" There's somebody coming at Christmas,
    you know."

GLOAMING.

THE setting sun has dropt below the
    sandy reach ;
The laggard rooks come home, belated,
    from the beach ;
Here in the garden-beds the flowers close
    their eyes,
And twilight's soft wan mist across the
    woodland lies.

O is not this most sweet of any time or
    hour,
After the garish day, and ere the night-
    clouds lower ?
'Tis as though Nature's self should pause
    upon her way,
Grey-clad and pilgrim-like, to meditate
    and pray.

MERMAIDS' VOICES.

THE golden moon peers through the rifted
      clouds,
    Now gleams the quiet sea,
And gentle winds unto our ears do bring
The songs that plaintive mermaids sing
    With mournful phantasy,
    And strange weird minstrelsy,
In magic caves beneath the echoing sea.

The moonbeams play upon the masts and
      shrouds,
    And bid the darkness flee,
And gentle voices in our ears do ring,

And songs that plaintive mermaids sing

  With mournful phantasy,

  And strange weird minstrelsy,

In magic caves beneath the echoing sea.

LARGO BAY.

"I cuist my line in Largo Bay."

Down by the shore, on a quiet summer
even,
All is silver grey, calm sea and shelving
sand;
Just a glimmering light shines over toward
Leven,
And a streak of azure lies on the southern
land.

Through the balmy air the plover's cry
falls shrilly,
Mingling with the measure of the slowly
rising tide;

G

Round the headland comes the white mist
weird and chilly,
Making nearness mystery, and distance
yet more wide.

By the salmon-nets a fisherman is bending:
Dark his boat and he in the twilight's
ghostly charm;
Whilst two lovers yonder, homeward
slowly wending,
O'er the grey-green links go, silent, arm-
in-arm.

TO A WHITE ROSE WITH PINK BUDS.

WHAT, is it so long,
Rose, since thou wert rosy,
Thy sweet mates among,
Press'd in clust'ring posy?

Art thou white for grief,
Wan because time passes
Fading every leaf,
Withering all the grasses?

Is it because age
Pales thy blush of dreaming,
Showing life's cold page
Unlike its first seeming?

Dost recal a wrong?
Or some past sad yearning?
Nightingale's love song
Gone beyond returning?

Dainty emblem thou—
Silence thy quaint meaning—
Why thy perfumed brow
Sorrowfully leaning?

Tell the secret hid
Deep in snowy chalice,
Tender petals 'mid,
Far from thorns and malice!

LAVENDER.

A PERFUM'D sprig of lavender
    You gave, dear child, to me;
It grew, you said, by the red rose bed,
    And under the jessamine tree.

'Twas sweet, ay, sweet from many things;
    But, (sweeter than all,) with scent
Of long past years and laughter and tears
    It to me was redolent.

A SUNSET SHELL.[1]

Sunset all in a shell?
The luminous West imprisoned
And held in the palm of your hand?
Yon mystic opalesque land,
The dream scarce a poet can tell,
Minimised, ay, rechristened
Here, in a sunset shell?

Just cast up by the sea
In the wet froth close to our seeking,
Painted clove-pink by the maids
Who dwell in the ocean shades,
A frail thing it seems to be,
With seaweed and brine yet reeking,
Here cast up by the sea.

[1] There is a small shell so named.

Is the sky under spell?
Nay, it may surely be wisest
Broad firmaments so to view,
Complete in tone and in hue.
Thy roof-tree's coloured full well,
Poor little mollusc that risest
Up on the grey sea swell!

Our world like thine is small;
Are we not made by one Maker?
And is the gold sunlight more
Than a perfect shell on the shore?
To Him who created all
An inch is as lov'd as an acre,
And the great the same as the small.

Perchance, as for whelks, to us
This planet's dark and half closèd;

Perchance on some walls outside

The reflex of heav'n is descried,

Or heaven itself, pure, rosied,

Is the converse of life spent thus.

IN THE LEA OF THE WIND.

'Tis pleasant to sit in the shelter,
When the wind whistles overhead,
And the leaves go helter-skelter,
(The leaves that are yellow and red,)
Whilst the green boughs that cling to the
    shuddering trees
Are whirling and swirling above in the
    breeze.

And sleep overcomes mine eyes,
As I sit and dream at noonday;
And the voice of the Future cries
In the blast, and it seems to say:
" Thou holdest thy life in thine hand, in
    thy will;
Thy life is immortal for good or for ill!"

THE SEASONS.

Spring and Summer bid the hills
With verdure be enfolden;
Autumn comes with lavish hand
To turn the green leaves golden;
Churlish Winter frowns, nor will
To any be beholden;
But strips gold glory from each tree,
Till woods and forests naked be.

SONGS OF LOVE.

(HER SONGS.)

THE FATE OF A SONG.

I MADE a foolish little song,
And sent it to my love one day.
O'er sea and lea 'twas borne along;
For he was far away.

Scarce was it sped when I betook
Myself to tears that it, not I,
Should touch his hand, and meet his look,
Or on his dear heart lie.

But when the summer came once more,
And we two trod the flowery mead;
Nor he nor I, our partings o'er,
Cared that poor song to read.

TO-DAY.

Is it to-day that I'll meet him? The trees
And the blossoms are answering "yes";
For Nature's kind self has joyfully donned
Her newest and loveliest dress,
And Zephyr with delicate finger weaves
My lov'd one's name in the rustling leaves.

Is it to-day that I'll see him? Ah me!
Fain would I be far more fair!
I long for the sea-depth to colour mine
      eyes,
And the sunbeams to garland my hair;
Yet this ignorant heart its joy cannot teach
To shine in my looks or ring in my speech.

Hark, how the thrush sings! It carols
    aloud,
With never a fear nor sigh;
Then why should I doubt? The glad-
    hearted flowers
And birds have less promise than I.
With the summer-warm noon my love
    speeds on his way;
'Tis to-day that I'll greet him—to-day, ay,
    to-day!

LOVE'S LITANY.

I AM longing for thee, dear, longing, O so
 wearily !
I am sighing for thee, dear, sighing, O so
 drearily !

I am mourning for thee, dear, mourning,
 O so sadly !
I am hoping for thee, dear, hoping, O so
 gladly !

I am yearning for thee, dear, yearning, O
 so truly !
I am waiting for thee, dear, waiting, O so
 duly !

I am pining for thee, dear, pining, O so
    lonely !
I am weeping for thee, dear, weeping for
    thee only.

I am sobbing for thee, dear, sobbing, O
    so wildly !
I am praying for thee, dear, patiently and
    mildly.

HESPER.

O FOR a light little boat,
  For you and me
  To go out to sea,
And float and drift, and drift and float
Through the sunset golden and red, afar
Unto the land of the evening star.

  When the sky is tender o'erhead,
   And the twilight still
   Creeps along the hill,
When the sun has dropt in his golden bed,
It shines with a brilliant light afar,
That mystic and wonderful evening star.

  And here, as we silently gaze,
   For ever doth rise

In my heart, in mine eyes,
A longing to climb those silver rays,
A longing to wander, hand in hand
With you, O my love, to that starry land!

WISHES.

In the meadows,
All among the meadows,
Where the yellow cowslips blow,—
There would I sing,
And weave me wreaths of all the flow'rs
that grow
Beneath the fragrant footsteps of the
Spring.

In the cornfields,
All among the cornfields,
Where the sheaves are red as gold,—
There would I be,
Where on a summer morn our love we
told
That made the world so very sweet to me.

By the rushes,

All among the rushes,

Where the cool green water flows,—

There would I rest,

And lay my weary head in chill repose,

And fold my tired hands upon my breast.

THE LILAC TREE.

I STOOD beneath the lilac tree,
  (O lilac tree! O lilac tree!)
It seemed my love came back to me,
  Once more to me, once more to me;
And from his eyes shone happy light,
And in his heart beat hopes as bright,
Ay, as when we, just I and he,
Held ancient tryst beneath that tree.

I dreamed beneath the lilac tree,
  (O lilac tree! O lilac tree!)
And in the future sought to see,
  To read and see, to read and see.
The chaffinch chirped behind the leaves,
The sparrow twittered from the eaves:
"What is 't to thee? What is 't to thee?
For that shall be must be, must be."

I wept beneath the lilac tree,

   (O lilac tree ! O lilac tree !)

I wot my love has gone from me,

   Gone far from me, yes, far from me.

The bleak wind bids the blossoms fall;

And yet my heart is held in thrall,

   (O lilac tree ! O lilac tree !)

As though my love were here with me !

A WOMAN'S PLEADING.

WHEN you're away,
My heart is sad ;
When you return
My heart grows glad.

When you are kind
The world seems bliss ;
When you are gay
I long for a kiss.

When you're distrest
I share your woe,
And when you weep
My salt tears flow.

But should you chide
I'd hang my head,
And if e'er you grow weary
I'll wish me dead !

MY HEART IS A LUTE.

ALAS, that my heart is a lute,
Whereon you have learn'd to play!
For a many years it was mute,
Until one summer's day
You took it, and touched it, and made it
      thrill,
And it thrills and throbs, and quivers still!

I had known you, dear, so long!
Yet my heart did not tell me why
It should burst one morn into song,
And wake to new life with a cry,
Like a babe that sees the light of the sun,
And for whom this great world has just
      begun.

Your lute is enshrined, cased in,

Kept close with love's magic key,

So no hand but yours can win

And wake it to minstrelsy ;

Yet leave it not silent too long, nor alone,

Lest the strings should break, and the
music be done.

FLOWER MESSAGE.

I'LL give my love a posy;
I'll pluck it e'en to-day,
Fair as my hopes, as rosy,
As tender, and as gay.

I'll send my love the garland
My faithful hands shall twine,
To give him in a far land
The sweet thoughts that are mine.

I'll make a chain of flowers,
Strong as a chain may be;
I'll weave with magic powers
And bind my love to me.

ONCE, ONCE UPON A TIME.

ONCE, once upon a time—
We were young, the world was new,
Love was fresh as morning dew—
It was long ago, you know,
    Dearest, long ago.

Once, once you took my hand—
" Little hand, hold tight the thread
Binding both our lives," you said—
It was long ago, you know,
    Dearest, long ago.

Once, once you stroked my hair—
"Who," you asked, "in all the world
Snares with net so golden-curl'd?"
It was long ago, you know,
    Dearest, long ago.

Once, once you kiss'd my cheek—
"Plighted troth thus fondly given
Ne'er is broke," you cried, "nor riven!"
It was long ago, you know,
    Dearest, long ago.

WOULD THAT MY HEART WERE
A SHIP!

MANY a day, dear, many a day,
Far and away, dear, far and away,
  My heart goes drifting to thee;
Would that my heart were a ship to sail
On a twilight eve, when the skies are pale,
  O'er the shimmering silent sea!

I'd guide her course by the light of the
    stars,
My loving thoughts should be ropes and
    spars,
  My truth should the ballast be.
I'd have fair Hope at the helm to steer,

And the skipper should be the Memory
  dear
  That draws my fond soul to thee.

And ay, that good ship should speed on
  her way,
And anchor at last in a quiet bay
  On the fringe of a sheltered strand;
Whilst gentle dreams should rock us to
  rest,
My harbour of refuge thy faithful breast,
  Thy heart, dear, my promised land.

LOVE CHANT.

WHEN we twain were young, dear,
We did not heed so much;
Love, on our hearts' fresh virginals,
Played with a careless touch.

Now we twain are old, dear,
Heart-strings seem tuned too high;
Life strikes a solemn chord thereon,
And then they break and die.

SONGS OF LOVE.

(HIS SONGS.)

O FOR A MINSTREL'S VOICE!

O FOR a minstrel's voice to sigh
In sweet refrain as my queen comes by !
O for a lute and a roundelay
To lull her to sleep on a summer's day !

My love she opens her lattice wide
To the brown-robed thrush that warbles
      outside ;
My lady she smiles at a beggar child,
But on me, alas ! hath she seldom smiled.

My love she kisses the red June rose
That close and fond by her casement
      blows ;
My lady she sings to the murmuring bee—
But never a song hath she sung for me.

O would that I were a pale moon ray,

At her window's lattice to linger and stay,

Or yon molten sunbeam that dares to

press

Her fair white brow in its glad caress !

MY LOVE IS LIKE THE SEA.

" Phillis is my only joy,
Faithless as the winds or seas. "
(Sir C. Sedley.)

My love is like the sea,

As changeful and as free ;

Sometimes she's angry, sometimes rough,

Yet oft she's smooth and calm enough—

Ay, much too calm for me.

My love is like the sky,

As distant and as high ;

Perchance she's kind, and fair, and bright,

Perchance she's stormy—tearful quite—

Alas ! I scarce know why.

For thus I'm tempest-toss'd,

A drifting skiff at most ;

I dare the waves, risk cloud and rain,

I ever tempt my fate again,

Nor care if I be lost.

DREAMLAND.

WILT thou come with me to Dreamland?
　　Dreamland lies over the sea;
We will float on a raft of poppies
　　That I have entwined for thee.

Wilt thou come with me to Dreamland?
　　It lies there beyond the hill;
Thou shalt travel, thy head on my shoulder,
　　Enwrapt in thy slumber still.

Wilt thou come with me to Dreamland?
　　The stars shall lend us their light,
Or the mystical pale Aurora
　　Shall guide our steps through the night.

Wilt thou come with me to Dreamland?
  With thy tenderest thoughts take wing,
And wander in yon fair kingdom,
  Where Love is the only king.

IF I HAD A CROWN.

IF I had a crown I would give it to thee—
A crown to encircle thy nut-brown hair—
I would say: "O fairest of all the fair!
I have made thee queen, come and dwell
    with me."

If I had a fortune I'd say to thee:
"Here is silver and gold to buy thee a
    gown;
Here are pearls for thy neck; let us go to
    the town,
And whatever doth please thee thine own
    shall be."

If I had a heart I would offer it thee—

A trophy to toy with, or haply to wear—

But mine has been broken in twain, I

declare,

By a thief that thou knowest who stole it

from me !

GOLDEN DAYS.

Sweet, remember
Golden days we spent together,
In the mellow autumn weather,
In the balmy bright September—
    Sweet, remember!

Sweet, forget them!
Youth and joy last not for ever;
When from golden days you sever,
Dearest, stay not to regret them—
    Sweet, forget them!

CHANGES.

WE sat among the cornfields, you and I,
The crimson sun was setting in the sea,
The sound of evening bells came o'er the
    lea—
I laughed a happy laugh; you sighed a
    sigh.

I mind me how the sunbeams kissed your
    hair,
The light wind fanned your cheek with
    fond caress,
Played in the warm folds of your soft white
    dress,
And singing birds proclaimed that you
    were fair.

Now we are parted, dear, yes, you and I,
With broad lands and wide seas betwixt
   us two;
I sit among the cornfields here, and you?
Perchance you laugh a happy laugh—I
   sigh.

DOUBTING.

NAY, do not ask me once again,
Thy very doubting gives me pain;
Have I not said? (and, while I speak,
Here's hand on hand, and cheek on
    cheek—)
    Dear heart, I love thee.

And yet, thy doubt to love allied
Is sweet, so sweet I dare not chide.
Cease not thy love, cease not thy doubt;
O child, I could not live without!
    Dear heart, I love thee.

For love 's not love that dreads no ill,
And doubt like this means loving still,

And both together fill thy heart,

To make thee lovely as thou art;

Dear heart, I love thee.

LOVER'S THOUGHTS.

I.

MAKE me a flower-bed like a heart,
  Plant a white lily therein,
Fence it with heart's-ease and lavender,
Just for the faith that I have in her
  Whom one day I may win.

There shall my lily be shrined apart,
  Fragrant with love and grace,
For thus, in the pleasaunce fair of my
      thought
Sweet-garlanded, tenderly, purely wrought,
  Shines out my lady's face.

II.

DEAR, when I protest
I'll give you leave to doubt me;
My silence fears no test,
My life may speak without me.

Those whose love 's least true
Most often seek to show it;
My love 's so great for you,
I care not you should know it.

III.

DEAR eyes so loving and so true,

I know not which is dearer,

The truth within those wells of blue,

Or love that shines yet clearer ;

For love on truth alone doth thrive and
feed,

And truth begets the love that 's love
indeed.

IV.

WHAT are my darling's eyes? They are
 blue as wild cornflowers.
What are my darling's looks? They are
 soft as summer hours.

What are my darling's lips? They are red
 as autumn roses.
What are my darling's smiles? They are
 sweet as springtide posies.

What are my darling's thoughts? They
 are pure as lambs in fold.
What is my darling's heart? 'Tis a treasure
 of pearl and gold.

What is my darling's soul? 'Tis a shrine
    where angels sing.
What is my darling's love? 'Tis a kingdom
    where I am king.

V.

If love might keep thee young, my sweet,
  Then shouldst thou be immortal;
Thou shouldst not age with years or grief,
  Nor pass through death's grim portal.

If love might keep thee fair, my sweet,
  No Grace should be so peerless;
Thy locks should never blanch with time,
  Thine eyes grow dim or cheerless.

But love can do no more than this:
  In life to love thee ever,
And when thou diest love thee still,
  And cease from loving never!

VI.

ONCE I was heart-sick, laden with such
grief
I called on Death to ease me of my
sorrow;
He answered not—but Love came on the
morrow,
And he, who'd wounded, gave my soul
relief.

VII.

As is one star, seen in a dark and murky
sky;

As is one flower that blooms upon a barren
lea;

As is a well of water, when all springs
are dry;

As is a ship, hail'd by a drowning soul at
sea;

As is the dawn unto the sick and ill at
ease;

As is sweet sleep to them that sad and
weary be;

As in the desert is a kind and gentle breeze—

So is thy love, my love, through all my
life to me!

A PAINTED MISSAL.

The other day I chanc'd to look

At the beautiful page of an ancient book.

'Twas painted in gold and in ultramarine,

Vermilion, and carmine, and tenderest

    green;

As fresh were the colours as though they'd

    been laid

On the vellum but yesterday—yet folks

    said

The work was just four centuries old.

Ah, man's outlived by madder and gold,

And time cannot stay like a parchment

    page

That carries God's story from age to age!

I gazed at the book as it lay on my knee;

Its dead world rose and surrounded me :

The years ebbed back, and to me it seemed

That in Florence I dwelt, and lived, not
    dreamed.

I walked through a garden I knew full
    well,

To seek one grave monk in his convent
    cell.

I passed down a path as familiar as sweet ;

I brushed the blue gentian with eager feet ;

I parted the lilies—and there I stood,

Awhile, at the fringe of the ilex wood.

In the belfry all the bells were asleep ;

From the porch one lay brother did vigil
    keep,

And yonder, across the warm white wall,

A lizard slid into the cypress tall.

I made my way up the broad stone stair,

Though many a white-robed monk was
  there ;
I gazed down into the cloister calm,
Where the west wind carried the citron's
  balm,
Where a young monk, burnished pail in
  hand,
Stood barefoot on the glittering sand,
Ready the water pure to draw
From a great stone well that I plainly saw
Under pomegranate trees, in a nook
'Mid vines that lay curl'd like a shepherd's
  crook.

This was the door ; it had bolt and bar,
But to-day it seemed to be just ajar.
I pushed it open, and entered the cell
Where my friend would be busy if all were
  well.

Ay, here he sat at the high oak desk,

Carved deep with many an arabesque :

A gaunt white figure 'gainst wall of white,

His austere face in a flood of light.

The light came streaming the window
       through—

A narrow streak of cerulean blue,

With a peep of the hills and the city that
       lay

Like a diamond bright in the keen midday.

The artist paused in his blazoned line.

The kind eyes were raised to encounter
       mine.

The pen was lifted, the work awhile

Put by ; the thin face warm'd with a
       smile.

Yet presently, as on the missal I gazed,

And tremblingly spoke, and anxiously
    praised,

One wan vein'd finger showed me the
    place

In the page, where the brush with its
    purple should trace

A chain of pansies my touch might now
    spill

On the breezy edge of the window sill,

And where butterflies, yellow as gold
    kingcup,

On yon painted rosebud to-morrow must
    sup.

And all adown ran the lettering fair :

Beati omnes in workmanship rare,

Scarlet initial that burned, as I read,

On the chrome like a poppy in summer
    corn bed ;

Gloria patri et filio, and then :

Spiritui sancto, whilst far down : *amen.*

And I looked and I looked, till the page
　　seemed to glow

Like a garden of glory where heaven's buds
　　blow,

Till a deep voice sighed softly : " Farewell,
　　O my son !

For life is but short, and my task is scarce
　　done,

And needs must I write ; through long
　　cycles to come,

This message shall speak when the scribe
　　has gone home.

Our hands are but human, yet art is
　　divine

If the glory of God shine through colour
　　and line."

❋　　　❋　　　❋　　　❋　　　❋

Then I woke. Lo, the book lay outspread
    on my knee!
But the monk in his cell could I never-
    more see.

TWO WAYS.

A MOTHER sang unto her babe:
"God's way is not our way," she said.
It seemed a lesson hard to teach,
That lesson which she daily read:
Too hard to tell a little child
Who sat upon her knee at play;
Too hard for life, too hard for love,
And yet—God's way is not our way!

The child grew fast, his step waxed firm,
Scarce any more was he a child;
And boyhood brought a thousand pranks.
Like others, he was rough and wild.
Yet for each mischance that befel,
Whilst many a tear the mother shed,

She pray'd him keep the narrow path :
"God's way is not our way," she said.

Man was he now, ay, all alone
To fray his progress through the world,
To keep heart pure, faith and hope high,
And his white banner hold unfurl'd.
Temptations thickened, closed around,
Yet, by a mother's spirit led,
He turned his back on golden sin :
"This way is not God's way," he said.

Then came misfortune—one by one
His nearest and his dearest died,
Borne from him 'spite his bitter tears,
Laid in the churchyard, side by side.
And as the mocking neighbours saw
Him sit aloof with bended head :

"Be this thy wisdom, Sir?" they cried.
"God's way is not our way," he said.

Next lost he fame, and name, and wealth,
And all the things men hold most dear,
So none to him spake kindly word,
And none to him would lend an ear.
Scarce had he pittance from a dole,
Scarce earned he daily drink or bread;
And yet, with meek and folded hands:
"God's way is not our way," he said.

Thus grew he old; ambitions pass'd
Above him—storm-clouds blown by wind.
Hope faded; vanished were all joys;
Content alone was left behind.
Suspicion touched him: "See, yon wretch,
A cur by fiends and witches fed!

Ill-omened wizard ! Cast him forth ! "
God's way is ofttimes hard to tread.

They took him, scourged him, stoned him
      till
The red blood gushed from every wound,
Till at their feet that martyr lay,
Fainting, dim-eyed, defenceless, bound.
He saw them not ; his joyful soul
Viewed heav'n that opened clear as day ;
God's angels sang, whilst his weak breath
Murmured : " Thy way shall be our way ! "

A LEGEND OF OLD.

In a green valley, nestling at the feet
Of mighty mountains—hid in blossoms
  sweet,
And fruiting chestnuts, and warm under-
  wood,
Beside a clear and purling stream—there
  stood
(Long ages since) from worldly turmoil
  shut
And screened aloof, a lowly, lonely hut,
Where dwelt a pious hermit.   There he
  pass'd
His blameless life ; the peaceful days ran
  fast,
Gathering to peaceful years above his head,

Like those white clouds that o'er the high
    peaks sped,
Drifting, snow-pure, and tinged by heaven's
    own light,
Close to God's sky, scarce within human
    sight.

Strange, as he weaker grew, by Time sore
    prest,
He added yet one duty to the rest :
Each evening, when the sunset fervour
    glowed
Upon the crags above, from rills that flowed
Beside his hut, the good man filled two
    jars
Of bubbling water, shining like the stars,
Cooling and slaking to all parching need ;
And these, for God's sweet glory, without
    meed

Or praise, he bore to the hill-top at night,
Though wellnigh fainting when he reached
  the height.
But there, where plants on arid rugged
  ground
Grew maimed and sere, where wild birds
  never found
The water-source they thirsted for, that gift
Was truly welcome ; down each gaping rift
The wondrous stream poured as 'twould
  never cease,
Whilst he, the giver, smiled in joy and
  peace.
Moreover, (for the Lord was pleased to see
Such patient tenderness and piety,)
An angel presence every waning day
Upheld the hermit on his arduous way,
Counting his steps ; one, whom the old
  man's eyes

Discerned, with wings outspread like flaming skies,
Kind strong-stretch'd arms, and pure en-
  raptured face
That turned earth's weariness to heav'n's
  best grace.
Then as, his task complete, the hermit
  drooped
Upon the hill-top, that bright angel
  stooped,
Kiss'd him, and brought him food, e'en as
  of yore
The ravens for the prophet fetched their
  store.

In garden plot once, while the recluse
  toiled,
He spied from far a miscreant, chained,
  torn, soiled,

Led to the gallows, pricked on, one for whom
(Whate'er his guilt) had come the blackest
    doom.
Down the green paths a rude tumultuous
    crowd
Gibed at the wretch, and marred with
    hootings loud
That calm-spread valley, where mild low-
    ing cows,
Sweet tuneful birds amid the whispering
    boughs,
Soft lapping ripples, all made harmony,
But human wrath jangled discordantly.
The hermit paused—a moment watched
    the sight—
Derisive sneered: "Ay, serves the villain
    right!"
Then turned to ply with zeal his rake and
    hoe,

Lest weeds around his favourite rose
    should grow.

That eve, when he had filled the jars,
    more great
Than erst unto the hermit seemed their
    weight.
He tottered as he went; the path was
    steep;
True, he had delved o'ermuch—he needed
    sleep.
Why tarried his kind angel? Sad his
    moan,
Wellnigh he wept. Alas, and thus alone,
Faint-hearted, he must dare the mountain's
    brow !
Gone was the daylight, dead the sunset
    glow;
Across the heavens the veil of twilight fell,

Grey, solemn, still, a weird and ghostly
spell,

Whilst o'er each rocky peak of violet

The fierce eye of a gleaming star was
set.

Through that long night all motionless he
lay,

Till darkness passed to dawn : then brake
the day ;

And down the hill-side stumbling, stiff with
pain,

Th' affrighted hermit sought his hut again.

There, on his knees, with hands outstretch'd on high,

Fasting he prayed, and rose his bitter cry ;

He searched his heart, eke as he asked the
Lord

How he had erred—whether by deed or
word—

Implored that, for th' unwitting sin for-
    given,
His humbled spirit might be duly shriven.
In vain. The angel came not. Pale he
    grew,
Dejected, worn with stripes and penance
    new;
Scarce could he stand; yet oft, in fitful
    mood
He crept with slow steps to the chestnut
    wood
Hard by.

      There, one morn, when the
    leaves were brown,
In meditation wrapt, he sat him down.
Sudden, from ruddy copse of autumn gold,
Flew out a bird, a sweet blue bird that
    told

Its gladness in so jubilant a strain
The hermit bent his head and wept for
     pain.
" Ah thou ! " he sobbed, " thou sing'st of
     joy, of grace ;
The Lord from thee hath never turned His
     face.
Sing, radiant bird ! Yet tell me how I'll win
Forgiveness for my deep-repented sin,
So **I,** like thee, light-hearted, free from
     blame,
May in glad cadence praise my God's
     great name ! "

Replied the bird with clear and noble
     song:
" Wrong hast thou done, yea, hard and
     cruel wrong !

A sinner poor and suffering thou didst
spurn,

Thy haughty soul did from his foul deeds
turn.

'Judgment is mine,' saith God: 'ven-
geance is mine.

'Tis mine alone—man! man! it is not
thine!'

Yet hearken, hermit: if thou grieve aright,

Through thine atonement darkness shall
grow light!"

Beside the bird an angel stood, down sent
To speak in words the hermit's punish-
ment:

" Behold this staff of ashen wood! Go, pace
The wide world o'er, and crave from place
to place

Thy bitter bread.   Take this dry staff—
>   by day
'Twill prove to thine uncertain steps a stay,
For sleep a plllow.   One short night alone,
In each house tarry thou.   Haste thee,
>   begone !
Bear hence the stave till from its stem
>   shall burst
Three green buds—then, be thou no more
>   accurst !"
The well-loved voice rang on the hermit's
>   ear ;
He listened, part in hope and part in fear,
Held out clasp'd trembling hands—the dry
>   staff they
Enclosed—th' angelic vision passed away.

Then back into the world which he had left

Long years ago, went that poor pilgrim,
    reft

Once more of riches, losing righteous
    mood,

Peace and self-praise, blest wealth of soli-
    tude,

And calm reflection—inward joys that be

Like props unto the soul's serenity.

He begged his way each day from door to
    door

Of grudging folk: with him the staff he
    bore,

Naught else, and, oft denied a crust of
    bread,

On his sad journey was he harshly sped;

Yet durst he ne'er complain. The staff
    was dry,

The snow lay thick; he turned with tear-
    ful eye

To homes he might not share, whence
    babes at play
Cried scoffing: "Hence, thou hoary head!
    Away!"

At last, from every threshold pushed or
    driven,
No crumb, no dole by any kind hand
    given,
As fell one cruel wintry eventide,
Within the forest was he fain to hide.
"Here," thought he, "shelter if not food
    may be,
So please the Lord, bestowed to-night on
    me."
He staggered on, bent double o'er his
    stave,
Helpless and weary till he reached a
    cave,

Where sat an aged crone.

"Good dame," he cried,
"Pity a wretch who in this world so wide
Finds naught of ruth. O prithee let me
    sleep!
My heart's sore laden, and mine anguish
    deep;
Dim are these eyes, infirm this trembling
    frame!
Have mercy!"

Thus he pleaded, but the dame
Quoth back: "Nay, nay!" Her cruel
    sons she feared;
Robbers, fierce men were they, who, as
    night neared,
Must sure return. Yet presently she
    gave

That boon the wanderer piteously did
    crave :
A narrow space beneath the rude stone
    stair,
To crouch upon and rest. He laid him
    there,
And pillowed on his staff his aching
    head.
("Twas meagre cushion, ay, and cheerless
    bed.)
Anent that cherished staff, much marvelling,
The woman asked and heard. Then did
    tears spring
From her eyes' fountains; sadly as she
    sighed,
Her mother-heart grew faint. "My sons !"
    she cried ;
" Poor heedless fellows ! If for one light
    word

This good man owns such suff'ring from
the Lord,
If of his righteousness naught counts for
gain,
Where shall your place be? What your
future pain?"

At midnight came the robber band; loud
laughed
Those brothers, revelled, cursed, threw
dice, wine quaffed.
But when the fire they lit leaped high and
glowed,
When a strange shadow on the white wall
showed:
"A spy! A traitor!" cried the angry
knaves,
Ready to fall on aught with spears and
staves.

Then the old mother: "Stay! A sinner
    he—
Weak, aged, worn—his penance doth he
    dree;
His burthen's heavy. . ." "Well said,"
    shouted they,
Kind from success in murd'rous raids that
    day.
" Bring forth the penitent—drink to him !
    So !
Greybeard, speak out! Thy sin we fain
    would know."

Up rose the hermit—strange his strength
    and new—
Nigh to the flaming logs he slowly drew.
Tall seemed his stature, his grand head
    scarce bent;

His eyes shone with his throbbing heart's
    intent,
As in the fireglow red he stood : " Yea,
    learn
How none may dare a fellow-creature .
    spurn ! "
Silent his listeners sat ; he told the tale
Of one who dwelt serene in sheltered vale,
And had for friend an angel wing'd with
    light—
Till, when one morn a wretch was hang'd
    in sight,
And he, the good man railed. . . .

             Ere he had done,
The robbers hid their faces ; one by one
They neared him softly—pale their looks—
    afraid,

Hushed, contrite, with unwonted tears each
      pray'd
The holy guest to shrive him; on their
      knees
Down fell they all, to earn their sins'
      release.

And when the saintly pity of his breast
Took as its own all heinous crimes confess'd,
Exhausted, now the pious deed was done,
He crept back to the couch so bravely won,
'Mid whispered blessing. All around, the
      night
Loomed chill and dark, the embers gave
      no light,
And in the cave reigned silence; scarcely
      sighed
The wind across shut casements.

That night died
The hermit. When blithe morning dawned,
the sun
Showed those who gazed that his hard task
was done.
As though in sleep he rested, with clos'd
eyes;
On his wan face a smile of glad surprise.
The withered hands were clasp'd, the tired
brow
Still leaned obedient on the staff, but now
'Twas crowned as for a victor's joy achieved.
Lo ! there a garland circled, fresh, green-
leaved;
Three buds, three boughs, had blossomed
from the rod,
To prove to men the mercy of their God !

N

CHISWICK PRESS:—C. WHITTINGHAM AND CO.,
TOOKS COURT, CHANCERY LANE.